That Can't

Be

Right!

Irreverent observations

full of possible notions

for coping with life

Carol Cook

Cover design by: Carol Cook and Print One Graphic Design

ISBN#: 978-1-7328019-0-5

Printed/Published in USA

Dedicated to

My Mother

Hilda 1920-2007

Table of Contents

*Printed in the Hood County News

^Printed in the AMAC Online Newsletter

Table of Contents – page 2

Lord, what fools these mortals be!
Shakespeare, A Midsummer Night's Dream

Introduction

Has the world shifted? Probably, which may be one reason half the people on earth are confused, some appear to be wandering aimlessly, others are coping; for the moment. Consider accepting those with odd, questionable behavior, or a bizarre attitude; for it's possible they are probably close to as normal as they'll get. Mind-boggling as it is, perhaps not all of us were meant to be competent.

So, excuse the perplexed and bumbling with an "Oh, bless their heart" outlook and the possibility they simply may not know any better, or they are managing with what is at hand. More than likely they don't handle our challenging world as good as others, deal with various failings, or figure out what's right or wrong. That's okay to a point, still, I'll pray the flawed, angry, and dumb people don't take over; I'm not sure I could handle ongoing doses of dim-wittedness, those who are constantly confused or causing some sort of trouble or uproar daily.

Humans are notorious for failure at something or other at any given time, so brush off imperfections with fun or happy excuses. Look at the positive, accept everything can't always be right. Chill; have a glass of Gods beverage, wine; and look at life as having an occasional thorn. Laugh at the unexplainable, enjoy the sparkling personalities, and the unpredictable.

Count the blessings we have and the people around us, know our pets love and need us and are always happy to see us. Feel fortunate we have hundreds of variations in coffee to drink, social media 24 hours a day, still have Dairy Queen ice cream after all these years, and if we drive far enough from the city we can see the stars in the heavens above. See, life is good.

The Joys and Woes of Working

Most of us aren't shamelessly rich where there is no need to be employed. However, nearly all that are rich got that way by working. This indicates the whole of mankind works for a variety of reasons, some beginning at a very young age, many studying for or spending great amounts of time learning a craft to keep them employed.

Working is usually to earn a living, what we love to do, for the heart of what can be accomplished, and for future yields. Indoors or outdoors, mothers raising children, soldier and sailor, fireman, police, consultants, and general labors. Our call or love of work covers as vast a description as fish in the sea, it keeps us going.

We may work for the predictable, the bewildered, a tyrant, or in chaos, yet for each job holder we're expected to be somewhere for a given length of time, accomplish tasks, produce results, and at the end of a day or night find something to feel good about. Still no job is exempt from muddling the mind.

If we are employed we're expected to get the job done. We're running a business, building highways, healing the sick, or tackling the complexities of daily production.

Working close or far from home in sometimes extraordinary conditions to receive payment for toiling vigorously, we're where we should be, or want to be.

Most, at some time in their working years, live with, deal with, ignore, and walk away from the complaint in the workplace, the confusion or helplessness. Some are relieved from their job and set about to seek a new or different employment. This of course brings on an entirely new set of requirements and rules for the working class.

Still they trudge on to put behind the anguish and desperation of not having a job, never grasping the idea of the carefree, do nothing, non-working class. While some unemployed are justified, possibly fired, some let go from restructuring of a business, others retired from long years of working.

Those who don't want employment can't grasp the tangled rules of working, some fall into categories such as incompetent, eccentric, or unskilled, others are just lazy. They simply don't want to work, which is a lame-brained idea to some, but the genuinely unwilling, under informed, or troublemakers have reasons for not entering the working rat race. Existing on eking out a living by hunting and gathering or mooching from others, including government handouts, is fine and suitable for certain breeds.

But work that is truly savored by the masses is usually joyful, needed and promotes self-worth; the idea of being productive has its positive side. It makes one happy and increases abilities at numerous tasks. Even our work foes have their use, bantering back and forth gives one a base for standards to deal with those who need war room railing and contradiction, rather like a chess game of work skills.

Working gives us our identity; it's appreciated, interesting, and fulfilling. A pay increase or promotion gives us a sense the day is justified, success is rewarding. The complainers were wrong; time moves forward, we are happily working, content accomplishing goals, and at best, gotten very good at shoveling.

My Umbrella Affair

With the onset of the rainy season it seems a good time to include the umbrella into a conversation. But why you ask, it's such a taken for granted, ho-hum item, easy to forget, lose, or break. Amazing as it sounds this genius invention was given to us by the Chinese in the 4th century, and with little change it's still used today.

Over the years, I've found them fascinating; possibly after my aunt gave me a lacy parasol when I was ten. I loved that frilly, miniature umbrella, which vanished over time; yet my enchantment with umbrellas lingered, growing into a unique collection.

When treated to the movie, "Singing in the Rain", starring Gene Kelly dancing across the screen, happily singing while soaking wet, I was smitten. I'm not sure if it was his cheerful spirit while singing in pouring rain or that I was simply dazzled by his dance with an umbrella.

In 1964 movie goers across the globe were spellbound when Mary Poppins floated over London with her magic umbrella and into our lives. Her enchanting umbrella had many wishing for one like it in hopes of floating away to anywhere they desired.

Drawn to umbrellas by their various shapes, colors, sizes, match a raincoat or boots, I kept several in my vehicle, office, and home. When I moved to England, the crème de la crème of umbrella land, I was in heaven. I bought traditional English black ones, different designs, fashionable, even sexy and odd ones were purchased for gifts and to keep.

Over the years I purchased uncountable umbrellas, including patio, beach, and golf, but the coolest one ever owned was confiscated by airport security. It had a flashlight and Swiss army type knife hidden in the handle, along with a wine opener attachment.

So naturally when I stumbled upon an article with umbrella facts I was challenged to look further into my attraction for them. I have no idea why someone would write about the umbrella, but it moved me to read about a well serving contraption I'd collected for years.

How intriguing to learn they are purchased worldwide upwards of 1.3 million daily, with approximately 900,000 a day lost, stolen, broken, or thrown away. Historical and famous characters have used the umbrella as a prop while the dictionary describes them as a protector from weather. On occasion during frightening moments they have been used to ward off threating characters, and as shown in films, James Bond has used them as weapons.

During a rainstorm people are heard saying they would give a hundred dollars for an umbrella. When one can't be opened during a downpour, or turns inside out in a storm, somersaults down the street like a tumble weed blown free, it usually triggers some rather colorful language.

When you think about it, umbrellas can be entertaining and comical. Often depicted in funny movie scenes, captivating to watch when someone beats theirs against an object, or when it's hopelessly chased blowing away.

I predict one day space exploring astronauts will be sent to investigate what is believed a newly discovered planet in the vast universe. Finding instead zillions of broken umbrellas all tangled together, floating along like a small planet held together with a trillion pairs of sunglasses, car and house keys. Buried inside the jumbled round mass are billions of TV remotes, cell phones, and garage door openers.

Watts Up

There's a lot going on these days that doesn't make sense, buying a lightbulb is one. It's true; have you bought a light bulb, any size, in the last year? Well, surprise, surprise.

There was once a time when we could walk into a store, buy a four pack of ordinary bulbs for the house and that was it. Bulbs for ceiling lights, lamps, the porch, anyplace we needed light. We can't do that today because the lightbulb industry has created a whole new type of confusion.

I will attempt to explain. All I needed was an appliance bulb for a five-year old refrigerator; why it burned out is a mystery because the bulb in mother's refrigerator lasted twenty years. It's not as if there are three teenagers spending thirty minutes each, six times a day, holding open the refrigerator door, yelling, "There is nothing in here to eat." This would of course shorten the life of a bulb, but the children are grown and gone now.

Fortunately, there are only six types of appliance bulbs, but to muddle our mind to the point of shock there is somewhere in the range of one jillion type of bulbs to light up everything, indoors or outdoors. It's possible a degree in electrical technology, or carry a guessing charm blessed by a leprechaun, would help a bulb encounter go easier.

Buying any bulb today is perplexing and difficult, actually, its mind altering, no matter what you want. Honestly, you will spend at least one hour searching, then thirty minutes with a sales person who has a badge labeled lighting specialist, and you still could come away with the wrong bulb. See what I mean.

Knowing the type bulb needed, what shade of light, wattage, how many lumens, and is it a halogen, or energy efficient. To be successful in your purchase, according to the lighting specialist, you should know if you need an LED long life, cool or warm, natural daylight, bright, soft, or white light.

Is it for indoor or outdoor use? Most everyone knows there is a huge difference; outdoor bulbs must be weather resistant, but are they for motion, solar, high intensity, high pressure, multi vapor, or flood, and what wattage is needed.

Watts for bulbs range from 8.5 to 500, buying the wrong watt could mean it could burst into flames. All this is rather exasperating for the buy-ee; so is the price charged for bulbs today. They may range from ninety-nine cents to $42.00 each! What is wrong with this? I remember buying a four pack of plain 100-watt bulbs for a dollar and they lasted all year!

Its possible bulb making companies has set out to confuse the masses, become a bit greedy, and laughing at the new language they created. That may not be exactly accurate, but it sounds as if capitalism might have a few flaws or else there are lighting engineers with too much time on their hands.

Our top priority is a light in the refrigerator; okay, through-out the house, the deck, patio, and the barn, of course the pool. However, we don't need everything to be lit up as bright and colorful as the solar system, but according to the electric bill, it is.

Mother, Mom, Mama, Mum

Key words that describe Mothers are many and varied, most often used are: Devoted, loving, overworked, tortured, housemaid, and slave to laundry. Far too many fit in categories such as the miserably tired, exasperated, sleep deprived, and at their wits end.

Of all the emotions moms know best its suffering, which is paramount for motherhood. Moms build misery blocking traits over the years through a series of on-going trails, mishaps and encounters with their children, their pets, and friends varied personalities, even the relatives.

Mothers are pacers, first with an infant then later when their teens do not return home by curfew time. They are professional sleep walkers during one, three, and five a.m. feedings of infant children, expertly trained stealth nose wipers, and kissers of boo-boo's. They are changers of diapers and healers of diaper rash, champion sugar-coaters and worriers along with being disenchanted cleaner uppers of spit up formula and strained peas, kid poop, spilled milk, and mud. Another title for moms is professional picker uppers from years of retrieving a thousand bikes left in the driveway and yard, a million toys, books, and items of clothing.

Moms are masters at promoting self-esteem and mending bruised hearts, harried champions at chauffeuring offspring to sports practice and games, music lessons, scout meetings, cheerleading, and band practice. She attends every recital, school fundraiser, and can recite every line of the school or church Christmas play. During summer she will make a thousand trips to the YMCA for swim classes and activities that resemble a disorganized boot camp.

Moms develop a keen sense for coordinating potty stops during car trips once they have left home, no matter the destination or length. She can also stop a vehicle on a dime when this statement is shouted out, "I can't hold it any longer". Plus, she can react as quickly as an emergency room staff, knowing all too well the sounds and signs of a vomit eruption coming on.

Moms are expert lie detectors, referees for sibling fights, and professional psychics and lip readers. They become the best correcting hairdressers and barbers for a child with gum in its hair or a trim done by its sibling.

Mothers have all the answers until their child reaches the age of thirteen; at that time moms begin to feel psychologically defeated because the child becomes a know it all. The responsibility of teaching tying shoe laces, brushing teeth before bed, hanging up clothes, and cleaning their room; most frightening of all, the teaching of driving a vehicle, usually falls upon moms. Duties that contribute to the graying of hair and frayed nerves.

They are survivors of dozens of slumber parties, along with ear splitting and nerve rattling garage band practices, each teen determined to become a rock star. A mother's emotions range from fear, joy, pride, despair, rage, and puzzlement, to exhaustion by the time their child is twelve; perplexed moms often ask, "What was I thinking".

A mother's prayers evolve from when she first holds her newborn, "Lord protect my baby" to "Jesus, please don't let me kill them" by the time they are teenagers, then to "Oh God, please help them finish school and get a job".

Mothers: First and fore most our best friend, our most ardent believer, protector, and supporter of dreams.

Clean Those Restaurants!

I've wondered from time to time just how clean are the restaurants we frequent; do they keep their kitchens spick and span and who's in charge of cleaning? I bring this up because most places I dine in don't appear as fresh and scrubbed as they could be.

I'm not Mrs. Clean on guard duty but I would like to eat in a clean place, unfortunately I've had occasion where I didn't feel I had. It's troubling to think owners and managers don't have as high a standard in restaurant kitchens as in their own home kitchen. So, the big questions are; why is the front door dirty, the floor sticky when walked across, why is dried food on the walls by the tables, and why are the menu's greasy-sticky feeling? This is just as troubling. Who's in charge of cleaning up after closing time?

It's possible a hurry-up, slosh a little water on things type of cleaner-upper crew rushing through a job without using grease cutting cleaners or scrubbing things spick and span is in charge. They tend to leave behind spilled and smeared food on salt and pepper shakers, ketchup and mustard bottles, on chairs, booth seats and backs, and the floor not scrubbed or mopped.

It's occurred to me that if a cook from a military mess hall, or my mother were at these restaurants when the clean-up crew arrived, there wouldn't be a problem with cleanliness. Moms see everything and military cooks in mess halls are detailed as a fierce drill sergeant; both constantly remind us that cleanliness is next to Godliness. The threat from either to put some elbow grease into cleaning or the promise their work will be inspected when finished might solve the left behind mucky-uck.

There are things that would make dining more pleasurable and managers would have fewer complains if chairs and tables were spotless clean, walls free of dried food, and floors sparkling clean, not a hint of sticky sugar-laden spilled drinks. This would be even better; not a single stray dried out French-fry, pickle, or tomato would be found under the tables either.

This is even more promising, with so much emphasis put on cleanliness we would no longer have to sit on vinyl and wood booths covered in greasy, spilled food that had turned to brown slime. This means we could be laughing, talking, enjoying our food and the joy of dining out instead of worrying what greasy-goop we were sitting in, touching, or if the kitchen was home to a whole colony of bugs, which I've personally encountered.

Mandatory rules for employees would make us all feel better too. Any worker suspected of being sick with a cold, flu, or virus, should stay home. Especially if they are coughing and sneezing onto people or food or blowing their nose while taking or delivering your order. Uck! This suggestion comes from experiencing a waitress blowing her nose, sneezing, and coughing as she took my order. I wasn't keen on having germs on my food or handled by someone obviously not well with who knows what kind of infection. Feeling threatened with germs and no longer hungry, I canceled my order and left.

Dining out elevates our mood, entertains us, and should leave us happy, but there can be encounters in restaurants that change our thoughts, mood, and brings about lifelong doubt of what is in the kitchen or how clean it is. My chance contact happened with a live roach planning to share my meal. I'm not kidding! The ordeal resembled a rehearsed comedy skit.

In a fine big city restaurant, I ordered a dish topped with hot cheese; it came artistically presented, the edge of the plate artfully adorned in green ruffled leaf kale; it looked luscious. As I picked up my fork an inch-long roach emerged from the greenery, stepped into the hot cheese and became stuck on the spot. Me, and my dinner companions, laid down our forks, the four of us expelled shocked groans as we watched the roach try to wiggle free. The unusual sounds of surprise shock brought the manager and waiter to witness the death of a roach in molten cheese.

The mortified manager quickly grabbed the plate and said, "I'll get another, your dinners are on us". The exchanged glances agreed, no thanks. We quickly exited the establishment, shocked over the weird experience, but once inside our vehicle all fell into fits of laughter.

Other encounters with live protein in my food, or odd creatures found at restaurants have made me a hesitant restaurant diner. An inch worm munching away on my salad and a snail in parsley arranged on my plate obliterated all desire to eat. Another was a comic event with a frightened, lost frog leaping from table to table, landing on diner's food at a restaurant's outdoor patio. But the most odd and scary, was a snake who had slithered up the side of an outdoor picnic table, peeking over the edge of the table top just as the potato salad was uncovered.

Dining out is always a joyful thought, no shopping for food, chopping, cooking, or washing up the dishes; it elevates the most ordinary meal. But with these quirky possibilities, creepy critters attempting to share our food, we have reasons for asking, "What is really in the kitchen and is anyone honestly cleaning up?"

Is Dumb the New Smart?

Older, wiser family offers guidance that is, at times, puzzling to younger members. Tidbits of advice is usually ignored, mystifying at the time, but later understand why they were spoken. Comments, warnings, or suggestions given during growing up years or at the time of family disputes were sometimes thought ridiculous, ignored. Later in life they became ah-ha moments that should have been taken seriously.

Traditionally spoken words were used as a base for principles for which were explained, advised as behavior, rules to follow. Parents and grandparents made comments that today might resemble a short therapy session. "Be careful of your words", "Don't count your chickens before they're hatched", "Pretty is as pretty does", "Don't Lie", "Don't live blissfully in ignorance", "Go ahead, make a fool of yourself."

Honestly, I don't think much of the advice given makes us any smarter, but it does make one pause, second guess yourself. Unfortunately, advice given that didn't sink in until it was usually too late to follow. Words to make one more aware of behavior, responses, and appearance doesn't always stick, still it's given to help develop or improve conduct and judgement, prepare one for responsibility, and maturity.

For some time now, no one has bothered with much of the giving of advice, which suggests, and creates doubts, possibly why we have issues with the younger generation. My concern and question today; is dumb considered the new smart? It seems this could be a reason for poor behavior, a lack of concern, thinking, and language.

Why bring this up? It seems there are a lot of ignorant sounding, downright stupid, behavior coming from what are believed to be smart people. Smart in the sense they have been raised in a working society with morals and values, spending years expanding their education.

I consider inventors, scientist, doctors, and astronauts as being intelligent. Smart from the goals set, pursued, accomplishments made, and the education level beyond college, along with their behavior in society. However, I've known several college-educated people who were just plain stupid, dense as a post in certain areas of knowledge to be precise. Behavior that appears to have slipped beyond reasoning, obvious a lack of common sense in some; today even more apparent among the younger generation with top notch educations.

It's annoying that people who appear to be intelligent, those held with highly regarded positions in the community, stray out of their way to do or say dumb things. They seem to believe it's the right, or a smart thing, even when they look the fool Shakespeare speaks of.

I don't understand what seemingly intelligent people are thinking when they disregard who they are; or who and what they represent. Questions aren't answered because they say it's difficult to answer, they're not good with numbers, or they can't give out that information without all the facts. Are they telling us they aren't as intelligent as we thought them to be.

Examples of this are government heads, i.e. Senate and Congress members; far too many city, state, and federal government employees, clergy, salespeople, financial advisors, and relatives; I could go on. Morals, values, and respect are lacking in so many we teeter on the defensive side more and more.

I'm also wondering if the people who keep saying, "You know what I mean", have no idea what they're talking about and simply want to put us in a position to agree we do know. They want us to believe they are smart, when in reality we know they might possibly be as dumb as they sound. Apparently, we reach this conclusion because that person is trying to prove they know what they're talking about, we know they don't.

I'll keep looking for signs the world isn't lost to stupidity yet, but its getting more difficult to hold an intelligent conversation with those younger than ourself. This leaves me to question just what is, or isn't, being taught in public schools for the past twenty years, and are we, the taxpayer getting our money's worth?

Shakespeare told us eons ago that, quote: "The fool doth (does) think he is wise, but the wise man knows him to be a fool". Another fitting quote is from Mark Twain, "Let us be thankful for the fools. But for them the rest of us could not succeed."

Maybe we should believe Darwin in his assessment, "All living things change as they adapt themselves to flourish or decline under the conditions they encounter". I'm just concerned intelligence isn't flourishing. Could it be on its way to becoming a thing of the past?

Foul Words

To what standards should we adhere if we speak foul words when annoyed or angered? Or, what do we do if words can't express a troubling time or explain a feeling and a need to complain about a situation or person? The smart approach for the user of foul words should be to first give thought and respect to the place they are in. They should also consider the fact everyone doesn't think what they are spouting out as acceptable everywhere. Filthy words and disrespectful language are often offensive to some who hear unpleasant words.

Unfortunately, most users of smutty language don't think their expressions are repulsive, which appears to be a shameful trend right now. Foul speech has become common for folks who have never been held accountable for their behavior, so they seek more attention by using vile or hateful language. They usually do this it in the presence of those who find it offensive and disrespectful apparently for some type pleasure for them self.

In all fairness, cussing can be fun, generations of sea going men are notorious for profanity, military service members use it frequently, sometimes as an outlet, possibly prove them self among peers. Cussing is a great attractor among the young wanting to sound grown-up, speaking gutter words gets attention, often brings on laughter.

However, some feel those who stoop to this level are to be excused for their ignorance and lack of class, others ignore their behavior, or laugh at their stupidity, or they're in agreement. Some are offended and comment what a terrible example to set for young citizens who hear such irresponsible rants and expressions.

The argument no other words express how they feel is their reasoning to vent, insult, shock. Most do not agree, thinking the more limited in vocabulary the user is by spouting foul words; this might mean their thinking is the greater the discharge of disgust it's possible the user will earn a type of standing by letting go with explosions of smut.

But then, all dreadful language isn't all bad for it depends on the setting. Some use of obscenity is harmless pleasure when used in certain setting with friends. Or it may be used for reckless graduating into adulthood, foul words whispered are often done to bring laughter, and at times these same words are an inexpensive pleasure shared with a group of cronies.

But there is a difference between vulgarity, disrespect and using a four-letter word when one stubs a toe on the footbed to one who continuously uses filth in public venues they're incomparable. Words used to express what is a feeling or happening by shocking with hurtful, obscene words, sometimes in a setting where they should not be used, are completely different.

Words that have been around way too long, beyond disrespect, are ethnic slurs hurled with indescribable distaste is beyond foul. The use of such hostile words sting, confuse, and undermine all that is good. They define the user as being lower-class minded, often poorly educated, lacking in vocabulary, downright mean, or possibly simply unaware of anything offensive.

There are those who believe they can speak or behave any way they wish, no matter the harm caused. They don't feel words hurt even when they see results that taunt. They have rights to express anything they so desire, how they want or think life should be, which is usually an excuse to themselves to hurt. Perhaps they do have those rights, but more important they should consider what my grandmother preached when one stepped on the rights of others. She spoke that those who thought they were forgotten or didn't fit in, wanted to be heard and seen, grasped at anything for attention to make a point, no matter the harm it could cause.

In retrospect, our world has changed, lost values along the way, drifted away from caring, often using pompous statements that simply don't sound true and right, and often aren't. But then who is in the right, or wrong? Still, my grandmother's motto rings wise: Use kindness, its noticed and heard, brings a goodness to any situation, sometimes stirs a quiet that feels right.

This may not work for everyone, every time, in all places, but it's a start.

Vacations

Everybody loves a vacation, a chance to travel, go anywhere planed or unplanned, even a quick get away from the ordinary is a great mind rest, a relief from routine. With all sorts of choices, places for a vacation, time set aside to get away, travel, see places, and do things that are interesting, leaves us open for plans to go amiss.

Every year when vacations are planned we have ideas of perfect places for reviving our body, spirit, and mind. With these dizzying thoughts of time away, a holiday for rest and relaxation, travel from daily living and working, or go somewhere different, we are captivated. But with all sorts of choices for a vacation, get away, time to travel, see places, do things that are interesting, which is not an easy undertaking. Everything doesn't simply fall into place because most of us aren't that good at planning.

Still we go, leave, determined to savor being someplace for leisure, enjoy the unfamiliar. We plan with assured success, yet fret, worry over the trivial; nonetheless, determined to fulfill our need for respite. Dreams for the stillness of a mountain retreat will satisfy, be unforgettable, long drawn out idleness, salt sea air of the beach, and sounds of breaking waves will call us over the years.

We anticipate the foreign, different cultures, the tastes and smells of exotic or diverse foods; curious what lies ahead. We look forward to, dream and plan for unusual and happy experiences, bask in the fantasy of being away from the ordinary, and revel with joy as soon as we leave our familiar place.

Upon arrival we unpack, settle in, and take in new surroundings, breathtaking scenery, sun and water, picture perfect weather, then fall into an easy, lazy state. We're ready to get out, explore, sightsee, eat, drink, partake of the unhurried leisure, and be entranced by the sights of the unusual, things we have joyfully left home for.

We're delighted with thoughts of the uniqueness in food, preparing our senses for varied tastes while someone else serves it, trying the exotic, and mixing rum and sun that leaves us dizzy with expectations. Or we dream of memorable encounters when empty wine bottles are left behind, cares are tossed, and we dismiss annoying insects, rain, and foreign language. No matter the bed we may sleep on isn't as comfortable as the one we left behind, we are somewhere exciting, happy to be anywhere away from duty and obligations, set on enjoying our gentle diversions.

Years from now we may have difficulty recalling the splendor of what was before us, encountered, the significance of it all. But for a few days we relish the different, the unusual, the history, even common flaws. We're entranced being somewhere remarkable, away on holiday, a tourist seizing each hour, each day to remember; the good or irksome of an experience.

And if we don't travel to the opposite we will never know the carefree adventures of our world, of foreign lands, a beach, lake or mountain retreat that could be mere miles from home. We will never know the annoyance of plans gone awry, language barriers, the boredom of mandatory museums and cathedrals, the ho-hum of monuments, or the joy of intriguing cultures.

The world can be mysterious, important, gritty and beautiful, so we should seek out its intrigue and wonders, the unique we yearn for in a place to travel. Places to be impressed, awe-stuck, or rest our body and mind for a brief, blissful recess.

When we return, we feel invigorated, enough to put the small pitfalls aside, lost luggage debacles, long lines; know we survived and managed our travel both delightful and challenging. Even if the photos don't convey the splendor we came upon, what we accomplished, or if it were for too brief a time away, we return to the ordinary of home with memories. We console ourselves with dreams of staying longer, relaxing more next time; wiser too, elated we've learned to pack less and lighter.

The Homeowner Effect

The season has arrived with a nudge to homeowners, the season for clean-up, repairs, and updates. For inspiration, a search begins for tools used during past motivational moments; when found, unfortunately, they don't work properly, are rusted, broken, or missing all together.

Almost everything needs fixing at some point and that is never more evident than when spring and summer arrive. Determined to take charge, clean the place up, and repair things that went unnoticed while we were comfortably in the chilled, lazy hibernation season of winter, we take stock of our home and lawn. With expectation we begin with list in hand, set off to the big box stores for tools and equipment, feeling assured of success, earn the title; jack of all trades.

Enthusiastic, likely motivated by TV fix up shows, and the possibility of saving a little money, how-to books for maintaining home and property are purchased. With heart racing, credit card ready, we acquire a fine set of tools to turn our home into a showplace. The joy of eliminating hiring, waiting for repairmen, landscapers, and those trained in fixing everything that constitutes keeping a home in tip-top shape, is exhilarating.

First, we begin self-training by pouring over how-to books on repairing a home, which is a must before any sensible do-it-yourselfer begins. However, we soon discover more tools, supplies, and paraphernalia will be needed. After acquiring such, its apparent our bank balance has become depleted.

But never mind, rumors will be quelled of being all thumbs, having brown thumbs, or having the most unkept property on the street; we move forward. The non-washing dishwasher, a leaky faucet, tattered and loose window screens, unsecured gutter downspouts, and the rotting wood deck will be repaired in no time.

The problem with a list of chores to be done is timing. It becomes evident things aren't going as planned or as outlined in the how-to books; more time will be needed. The drill purchased was the wrong size for the job and several items scheduled for repair were not designed to be fixed; which confirms we really are a throw-away society. If something doesn't work to one's expectations, or breaks, its thrown away.

After what seems a thousand man-hours, exhausted, sunburned, scrapes, cuts, bruises, the extraction of thorns, and all patience eroded, only a quarter of our goals have been reached. Realization sets in; it's not possible to fix a thirty-five-year old Harvest Gold dishwasher, replace loose roof tiles using a six-foot ladder, or rid the property of fire ants without experiencing dozens of stinging bites. Plus, taking this advice could save a bunch of money on repairs, or save a marriage; any tree trimming or cutting should be left to a tree service.

Landscapers, plumbers, electricians, and carpenters love do-it-yourselfers, it's good for business when novices and penny-pinchers take on repair plans. However, they do suggest if a screwdriver, hammer, chain-saw, or ladder is used, it's important to exercise a little common sense and caution when wielding either. Reason, the National Safety Commission reports that emergency rooms across the land treat on average 36,000 injuries a year from homeowners attempting repairs on their property.

A variety of personalities and talent's make up homeowners, but common words heard most often from nearly every spouse of the "I can do-it-myself" homeowner as soon as an injury occurs, "See, I told you so".

The Great Flush

Some of life's greatest pleasures are small and lie readily at reach. They can be ho-hum or pure joy. But everyone will agree, some privately, that an effortless push of a handle to flush a toilet might fluctuate between bland and happy when put in a category of pleasures.

You ask, why is the subject of flushing a toilet being brought up, or compared to small pleasures? Truthfully, this is an educational offering for those like me, a homeowner faced with worry over a plumbing problem, an issue with the government, and the amount of water I can use to flush my toilet.

And you say, "Who cares". Until you are faced with this, you wouldn't, but here are the facts. Our home toilets don't last forever; they leak, wear out, and become plumbing disasters, moving one, no pun intended, to set about the chore of purchasing a new one.

But as we know, toilet speak is not something people usually get together to discuss. But an indoor, flushing toilet is something significantly important to each of us. If you don't believe me, try living a few days with a non-working one.

The used every day device in my home was circa 1970's and sounded like a rushing waterfall dropping fifty feet onto a river when it was flushed. A slow leak dripped constantly, plus it required five gallons of water to enact a flush; a waste of water the ecologists remind us. Well, by today's standards they're right, but the toilet was old, worn out, and needed replacing for it worked only sporadically, which is not a device you want to work only part time. The plumber's words of advice regarding the porcelain throne; there is no fix for this, buy a new one.

If shopping for a toilet hasn't been on your to-do list for the last 10 years, you are in for a surprise and will become quite perplexed when you actually "must" partake of such an experience. I didn't know they came in various styles just as refrigerators do with approximately twenty different types to choose from. But the biggest surprise, the government has a say in what type toilet we install in our home, and how much water we can use to flush it. Upon learning this I said to the store clerk, "You can't be serious"?

To be environmentally correct today we are required to install low-flow toilets with an efficient flushing system to please our law makers and save our water resources. Yep, our rights have been flushed with 1.6 gallons of water! However, the most bewildering task; find a suitable toilet for our home and size family.

There is the standard low flow, a high performance one, or gravity assisted or syphon action flushing type. Choose the wide flapper valve for better flushing or stay with the regular two-inch valve. Select the sleek skirted trap way design, a round or elongated style with a purist look, or opt for a single or dual flush.

We can choose porcelain white or cream, or various colors for a price, one with modern subtle curves and clean lines, or with sleek symmetry. There is also a choice for a push button flusher or a left or right handle flusher. Then a decision has to be made on the type seat; a quiet close seat or a regular seat; or consider adding a lighted seat option. See what I mean!

Oh Lord in heaven I pray, protect our bathrooms from the government toilet police, the ecology nuts, and those dufus Congress humans from enacting anymore rules for our commodes, the john, the throne, or as the British refer to it, the loo. Whatever we call it, please pray the environmentalist are finally satisfied.

Twist and Shout

What is it with manufactures who put their products into sealed packages we can't get out unless the equivalent of a hatchet is used to pry them open? Nearly everything we buy is wrapped or sealed in protective covering to the point we spend twenty minutes trying to get it free from its tomb!

You know what I'm talking about! Items in the grocery store, drug store, department stores, and home improvement stores are near impossible to get open. Why have manufactures made things so difficult for us? It's possible it has something to do with government regulations, or a shop lifting deterrent, either way, it's annoying.

Hearing others complain tells me I'm not the only person grumbling or trying various techniques in the attempt to get something opened and out of a package. From what I can determine, since some nut case secretly put poison inside aspirin bottles for the general public to buy and die from ingesting, everything is sealed up tighter than a space craft headed for Mars!

To open a package of sliced sandwich meat today we need a pair of scissors or a box cutter knife to get the pressure sealed plastic casing open to retrieve a slice of turkey or ham for a sandwich. A slice of cheese, same thing, hot dogs, bacon, anything in a box, frozen container, and items from the deli.

Buying anything from the pharmacy aisle; a toothbrush, package of razors, a bottle of anti-acids, mascara, or cold medication takes approximately ten minutes to open, it's ridiculous! If we shop the cracker and cookie aisle, same thing, plus each box of either comes in at least two wrappings. First is a cardboard box, inside is an airtight, plastic type cellophane with the cookies, crackers, cereal, or rice. To get that open one needs the strength of a weight lifter to pull it apart; or resort to taking a pair of scissors to cut through to retrieve the product.

Most things we buy are sealed in decorative or colorfully designed packages so the item will be more appealing to a prospective buyer. That is fine and good but when one tries to open it, either a pair of scissors or a box knife is needed; even resorting to using a pair of pliers is another alternative to get a container or package open.

Try getting the lid off any bottle of pills, which have obviously been mis-labeled as child proof, how about a label that states it is adult and weight lifter proof! I don't know any adult that can get the lid off a bottle of prescription pills, or the pull tab under the lid of dish washing liquid, and the salad dressing bottle requires a knife to pierce the plastic seal.

Squeeze the lid and push down at the same time you are also required to twist, or pull, are the most annoying instructions for removing a lid ever experienced. The manufactures expect everyone to have perfect eye-hand coordination, not to mention the strength of a gladiator! Getting a product open that has been sealed by a machine simply can't be done by a person.

Who do the manufactures think is going to open them? Well Jack the Giant or an Olympian weight lifter won't be around to use sheer brute force to get the bottle of ketchup or a package of flashlight batteries open. Perhaps stores selling anything sealed in industrial strength plastic should have an employee, or robot, at the door to open your product(s) before you leave!

Unscrewing a lid from a jar of pickles, a bottle of mouth wash, and a hundred other items with a lid or cap is an all-time frustrating nuisance. It's near impossible to remove a lid without banging it onto a counter, running hot water over it, or the twist-ee screaming out words that should not be heard by children, and swearing it's going to take a hammer or garden shears to get this thing open.

What are product testers thinking, who know opening it might be a problem yet do nothing about it. Do they really believe anything screwed on or capped by a machine in assembly lines can be easily taken off by a human? Especially those who aren't into strength training.

And it isn't just lid's that can't be opened; someone invented the impossible juice and milk carton with instruction to cut or pull here, tear this tab; they do not tear or open here at all. It takes a screwdriver or scissors to pry open or cut the seal, which leads me to believe industrial strength tape or glue has been used to seal it up. Products such as batteries and packages of tape, any product for the office, all are sealed in a material that is used to make sure every crevice on a NASA spacecraft is airtight.

What next will be sealed in super strength, space age material? If it's our food we could all suffer from starvation because we can't get the product open. Could this be a new diet plan?

Bargain Shopper

Bargain buying has changed the definition of a good purchase, finding sales, close outs, anything marked down gives us satisfaction. It was 50% off, a real steal, what a bargain! Words most of us happily speak. Apparently, its a deal hunter's goal to acquire anything on sale that is needed, wanted, entertains, or makes one happy; sometimes purchasing stuff simply because it's on sale, needed or not.

Everyone loves a sale, a good value for the price, be they a shopping expert or regular shopper buying what is needed. Some are out there to get a deal on every item for the home or for them self, supporting the rumor shopping is a favorite pastime of the human race. Only football and golf might be considered its closest rivals.

Over time, mankind, womankind actually, has been shopping and gathering, searching for bargains and deals on everything from food, clothing, trinkets, and places to dwell for ieons; then filling the home-place with furnishing and comfort. Buying what entices us, entertains us, makes us secure, or what we think is needed has become the world's most popular activity.

Women are shoppers, competitive, driven when it comes to finding everything she and her family could possibly ever need or use. Across time, buying things became a necessity, getting anything at a miserly price has been a stimulator, rousing us in the ongoing search of a deal, great bargain, any transaction at irresistible prices.

When the shopping mall came along we were transformed, for better or worse, in youth and beyond, this gigantic haven changed lives. Filled with practically every product known to mankind it gluttonized a need at every social level, provided us with entertainment, and saved us from boredom. Unfortunately, it created impulse buying and debt.

These sprawling retreats, free to enter, warm or cool inside, are also educational. The chance to discover what is new to the world was an eye-opening and enlightening diversion in our everyday life. Its magical location offered a place to eat, socialize, take in a movie, exercise, and much more. The human race was hooked.

Whole cities of people became explorers searching for the unique, hunted for mass produced merchandise, gadgets, things we believed were must have's, discovering a world of things we didn't know we needed until our eyes fell upon them. Gathering the ridiculous, the unneeded, and buying recklessly often pushed one to the edge of shocking debt, sometimes filled our conscience with guilt, even in a pleasurable way.

Yet, as deal searchers we also succumbed to land buys, auto negotiations and trades. We gambled with the stock market, found bargains at markets, outlets, and became obsessed for travel and vacation savings. Drawn in daily to beckoning sales of electronic, home improvement, and television buying stores moved us to the point we became professional buyers, hagglers, collectors, and cheaters.

Once a certain age has been reached, some get past the need to buy, collect, or bargain hunt, but the new-age shopping utopia that has captivated us, taken us hostage, is internet shopping. Labeled as the new breed of shoppers, value seekers, deal traders, and collectors, this cutting edge buying, browsing, and dreaming has emerged as a fix for the shopaholic.

It's an exciting paradise pulling us in as if by hypnotic trance, transporting us to a buyer's Shangri-la. It's a happy, fabulous place to acquire your hearts-desire, anything for happiness can be bought in the form of vacation escapes, everything in the tech world can be ours, along with any type food, clothing, vehicle, toy, tool, cosmetic, name it, it is on line to buy. All can be done, acquired while sitting poolside, on the beach, in an airplane, or lounging comfortably in pajamas at home.

When the birds are singing, it's not a requirement to buy them, simply sit back, enjoy, and listen because they'll be there every day, for free. No purchase is necessary.

The Weather Is Frightful

It's supposed to be winter; cold, harsh winds, a hint of snow flurries, wood burning in fireplaces, coats, gloves, hats at the ready, all eyes glued to the TV weather channel. But it's not winter, it's a season with no name, rather like an imaginary season, which is rather confusing.

Winters in the South consist of several days of cold temperatures; we turn the heater up to near broil and bundle up as if headed out for a Mount Everest expedition. Within hours the weather shifts with the wind and air conditioners turned to freeze-out mode. People are wearing tank tops and flip-flops, eating a curl top ice cream cone, and driving around with the windows down like its spring.

The few winter months in the lower half of the USA leave us perplexed if we take time to listen to weather forecasts. The weather team shouts out warning of falling temperatures, a possible freeze, and a chance of snow, but their predictions seldom come true. If temperatures fall to freezing we hunker down for a few hours until the weather channel gives us news the next day will reach seventy degrees, sunny with possible sightings of daffodils; even a few mosquitos might congregate.

Northerners are seen on national news and weather channels scraping ice from windshields, sliding around on roadways, and toiling for days digging vehicles out from under snow. Snow plows prowl streets moving snow and ice for days on end as electricians repair ice covered broken lines. Residents grumble over power outages, frozen water pipes, and frostbite while southerners sit in their recliner shaking heads at these antics, sipping on iced sweet tea.

But these winter lovers are a happy lot, some hold themselves superior to warm weather loving folks by referring to them as weather wimps. They laugh and point fingers when Southerners shiver in heavy coats if the temperature drops below fifty-degrees, completely out of their element if snow flurries fly for twenty minutes. But, heaven help them if it should sleet.

Winter loving folks tend to wring every minute of fun out of their bone chilling weather; they play in freezing temperatures skiing, sledding, ice skating, and ice fishing, which doesn't sound normal to me. They tell us it's healthier if one is outdoors in zero-degree air, chopping wood or shoveling snow from their frozen tundra.

Cold weather lovers speak of hundreds of songs written about winter, gloat they have the winter Olympics, jam-packed ski resorts, the famous Iditarod sled race, and their football teams can win a game in zero temperatures with snow or sleet on the playing field. They tease and crow Southern teams can't even hold a frozen ball and could only win a game if divine intervention happens.

The trouble with winter in the north; its' cold and miserable, stops dead as if in a coma, doesn't move for months. Bare trees and gray skies can put one in a gloom-mope-around mood, the snowed in blues for weeks on end while in the south the daffodils are sprouting.

It doesn't sound natural to have temperatures at minus twenty any more than it does to live with a hundred-degree summer cooled with air conditioning turned to sixty. Although, have you ever heard anyone in the south speak of what a wonderful winter it was and where did it go

Sunsets and sunrises are more than likely just as breathtaking in the north as they are in the south; but there is a question circulating. Why is there a Southern Living magazine touting the joy of living in the South but not one for Northern Living?

What Is That Smell?

What is that smell? Whatever it is, it's going to be either good or bad when someone asks; "Ohhhhooo what is that wonderful smell, or, Oh Lord what is that awful stink".

The old saying the nose knows is true. Human ability to smell is explained by researchers as the most primal of man's five senses. We have a sensibility toward scents, a role our brain processes continuously to detect scents. Studies show our mood, energy, emotions, eating habits, how we behave, and more are affected by scent.

Think about it. Fresh cut grass will take us to our childhood play time outside in the summer. The smell of popcorn, corndogs, diesel fuel transports us to good, fun times, or a long-ago time. Perhaps our trip to the fair with the Ferris wheel oily smell, the heavenly scents of food we can only get at a county or state fair.

A stinky ordeal will also stay with us what seems forever. The year the dog was sprayed by a skunk is branded in our brain, and the stink of driving past the paper mill fills our vehicle with such rotten of smells we gag. The scent of blooming flowers during a tour of the botanical gardens puts us in the happiest, most uplifting of moods.

An experience on a crowded elevator with body odors, perfumes, after shave, and garlic breath may cause us to sneeze, cough, gasp for breath, and pray the elevator doesn't break down. However, the worse smell that lingers in our nose forever takes place on elevators. It happens when someone let's go with a breath taking away release of gas, nearly gagging anyone in the elevator!

Heavenly scents of apple pie baking, a turkey roasting at Thanksgiving elevates our mood to extreme pleasure. The scent of cinnamon, pine, and fresh snow will forever linger as the most memorable scents of Christmas time. Walk into any restaurant with the smell of bacon, sausage, and coffee and we are home again, with mom, grandma, or a favorite aunt.

Coffee is one of the most desired of scents, and taste, especially first thing in the morning to wake up our mind and body. The scent of coffee in exotic or foreign places will stay with us long after the experience, triggering memorable of times.

The most enjoyable cup of coffee I have ever experienced, an aroma strong and earthy, almost hypnotic, was served one spring morning at a sidewalk café in Paris, France. It was the best coffee I'd ever smelled or tasted. It's possible the memory of where I was played a part in keeping the scent and taste forever locked in memory. No matter, the memory is delightful forty years later.

Smells from childhood linger a lifetime, so will holiday meals with intoxicating aromas. Brownies, cookies, pies, and cakes baking; campfire meals and roasting marshmallows keep us mesmerized. Bar-b-que meals and scents of anything grilled outdoors tantalizes us; soup simmering, fried chicken, and anything cooking at the fair.

I'm not sure if this is scientific fact or not but women can smell better than men, they do most of the shopping and cooking, so they smell and sniff out everything. They also sniff food they take out of the refrigerator, if it smells suspicious, it's thrown away. Men will eat most anything, even when the expiration date expired last year.

Take time to sniff out the good smells, elevate your mood, smell the flowers, lavender, jasmine, honeysuckle, a fresh powdered baby held close, a wood burning fire, new car, fresh clean air, the scent of rain, and fresh growing herbs . Partake of the fragrance that will improve your thoughts, help you rest or sleep, and leaves a good feeling,

However, what may appeal to one person's nose may offend another, triggering sneezing to those allergic to certain scents, especially chemical smells and perfumes. Odors that give us an oh-no are burned food, cat litter boxes, and smelly gym shorts and shoes.

Think of scent as the most primal of our five senses, originally it helped us seek out food and detect danger, even find a mate. Today we often think of smell as a form of comfort especially with the scent of flowers, spices, and sugary desserts. Even an herb garden, small or large gives off scents to make us happy, improve our food, and overall create a feeling of well-being.

So be happy, plant flowers, buy flowers, plant an herb garden or buy them to cook with and fill your home with wonderful smells. Listen to your brain, breathe in the heavenly scent of just baked nose-tickling brownie that smells wonderful, oozing chocolate, which is good for the soul, dangerous for your weight, eat it, you'll feel great.

Driving Modern Roadways

Every year more drivers are added to our highways, this only compounds the confusion of dodging untrained drivers, vacationers, and tourist from other states and countries. It's apparent this situation makes daily driving a mind-altering experience when the masses set off to anywhere. However, a few reminders and explanations could ease these increasing and trying encounters, at least help us cope. Or hopefully avoid menacing nincompoops who aren't even qualified to drive a golf cart.

Difficult as it is, what I'm about to reveal is true. If you do much driving, you may have noticed traveling any distance by automobile has become akin to participating in hand to hand combat. Why is this? It appears there is a new breed of driver on the roads who are either angry, dead dog tired, overworked, or just plain careless and don't care if they follow the rules or not.

You may have noticed, strange as this seems, drivers are in a state of road rage, work rage, parking lot rage, construction rage, and who knows what else has driven them to these ranting and insane moods. This is an unproven theory, but someone should at least try to explain the cockeyed reasoning behind such slip shod driving.

Recently, a report revealed a huge percent of drivers are speeding no matter where they drive. This causes others, those following the rules, to be struck with fear, then a dumbfounded type of disbelief takes over and by the time we return home we're mumbling to our self. Sometimes we're numb, cursing, or shaken from our brush with death, definitely in need of a shot of whiskey, or find ourselves swearing to give up driving.

This is another serious issue today; there are people on the road who haven't, or can't past a driving test, even after three tries, some won't pay the fees required to get a license or insurance, yet they drive anyhow. Then there is a frightening group who are new to America and simply get in a vehicle and drive, without ever having read a driving instruction manual; plus, they can't read a single road sign.

This could be the reasoning why a tiny minority of law-abiding citizens who are conscientious, drive safely, and obey the rules of our roadways feel threatened. Crazed drivers waving their arms as if having a seizure, tailgaters, and what appears lobotomy patients, are driving 90 mph as they weave about the road. Others attempt passing on the right shoulder of the road or act as if they've never been in control of a moving vehicle. Nearly as frightening are stressed-out working mothers leaving grocery stores, suffering from shocking prices, wobbly cart annoyance, waiting in line rage, and slow check-out lane rage, then dashing through traffic to pick up the kids in less than three minutes.

Perhaps this may answer annoying questions of why there are so many crappy drivers today. It's also possible those mentioned want to be somewhere other than on the road and want to get off it as soon as possible. They flit about the road like mosquitos, don't bother to stop at stop signs, yield signs, or pay attention to traffic lights. Some are chattering away on a cell phone, eating, applying make-up, or shouting at children. Nor do they wait for a left turn arrow, instead turning quickly in front of oncoming traffic, believing waiting for a green turn arrow is for slowpokes.

I'm willing to bet three-fourths of those making a turn have no idea a turn signal lever is on the left side of their steering wheel either, and they zip past stop signs as if they weren't there. For the scared to death, cautious driver, prayer might help ease the mind while on the roadways, but then that could also be a flip of the coin chance.

Another problem with drivers; a large percentage are color blind! I'm not kidding, which is absolutely a horrifying statistic, proving most people never see a red or yellow traffic light! The only color they recognize is green! This means the *follow the rules drivers* are dodging lunatics every day, hazards we desperately need solutions for. Then, the entire country is under construction, seriously. Every city street, roadway, interstate, and major highway is as challenging to get on or through as attempting to drive through the Amazon jungle in a 1975 Ford Pinto.

A great number of vehicle owners don't know this rule either, or if they do they ignore it. It's actually a safety measure and simple common sense. Turn the vehicle headlights on when it's raining, foggy, sleeting, snowing, or if it's just getting dusk. How drivers don't grasp this helps them see better is a mystery!

I sincerely believe a lot of drivers on the roadways are empty-headed dummies, never think about what they are doing or where they're going; but, try driving in Europe or Asia; which isn't for the faint of heart. The Italians drive in city streets at 60/70 miles an hour as if the world will end in fifteen minutes, so do the Greeks. I won't even attempt to describe the French or German drivers, even the once polite British drive like madmen; it must be something in the water!

This is an annoying driving habit the Europeans have, which is baffling. They are chronic horn honkers which makes the entire continent of Europe continuously filled with horn sounds reverberating off every building, bridge, and cell tower on the continent. My concern, the aliens tooling around in their space craft hear the on-going, annoying sounds of honking and refuse to stop for visits anymore. I'm sure the remaining countries around the world have their share of incompetent and psycho drivers but I don't even want to speculate why.

At this point of concern what I'm about to reveal in a confession is frightening. I've been in six car accidents, yet was never responsible for any of them. It was other drivers who were careless, simply ran into my vehicles.

The sad outcome of this is learning three of those accidents happened when I was stopped at a stop sign and at a red traffic light. The other three happened when driving carefully, following the rules, and the speed limit.

This could suggest I was the dangerous driver because safe driving rules were practiced.

Can You Read the Small Print?

Can you read one word on your prescription medication bottle? I can't. I can't read the name of the medicine, directions, how much to take, or the expiration date because the print is so small a magnifying glass is needed to read it.

The doctors name, phone number, when the prescription can be refilled, and any warnings is also printed so small it's a blur. Any possible adverse and allergic reactions can't be made out either, nor the name of the manufacture; all in such microscopic print it's unreadable by the human eye. Why is this?

Not one word of information printed in fourteen languages on a tiny slip of paper folded in the box with the medicine makes any sense. It too is in such miniscule print it's pointless to try reading it; even the one printed in English!

This is annoying to millions taking medication for whatever ails them. Not a word can be read how much to take or how often, its maddening. How many pills are to be taken? Two every four hours or one every hour? Who knows? Not a word can be read without glasses.

I've reached an age, like my friends, where I need reading glasses. I hate that I need them, which are never in the spot I thought I left them. If I go shopping I can't read the ingredients on a box or bottle on anything from crackers to shampoo!

If I want to read the label on clothing in a store, the price tag or size, I must dig in my purse for reading glasses. I can't read the instructions for use on anything new I purchase, nor in what country the item is made because it's in such itsy-bitty print. It's now impossible to sit back and read a novel, the newspaper, or a magazine, nor can I work on a computer, I-pad, do a crossword puzzle, or see the playing cards without reading glasses.

Even going out to eat is aggravating for it too requires reading glasses because menus must have been printed for Leprechauns. I can't see phone numbers on business cards, or who's card I'm holding. I can't see who my mail is from, and notes left for me to call so and so also requires I don my glasses; I feel I've lost contact with everyday reality because I'm blind as a bat!

This has put me in such a bothersome place where if I ever want to see anything printed, or look up anything, I'll forever need those dang glasses. This is just as annoying.

What will I do if I travel in an area I can't get a signal for GPS? I'll never be able to find where I'm going because maps are also printed in teeny-tiny print!

This is probably the most annoying, even my girlfriends are complaining. A magnifying mirror is needed to apply make-up, mascara, and lipstick as well as apply hairspray. Plus, I'll forever have to keep a pair of glasses with my cosmetics and use a 10x make-up mirror to see how I'm applying all of it.

Reading is bliss, educational, a time out get-away; my entire life has depended on it! Now, I'll have to shop for books that are printed in large print. Seems as if my life revolves around my reading glasses, if I can remember where I left them!

Believe it or not I was once cool, now I'm feeling uncool using readers to see any and everything. But the biggest downer is using reading glasses to see the D for putting the car in motion, that is a perfect example of uncool!

Going to The Movies

It's a shame many of us don't go to the movies like we once did for it gave us great joy and memories. Unfortunately, there is a feeling among us today our film industry has changed to something beyond entertainment; spewing foul language we would never consider using our self. Most scenes in movies today are filled with smut and violence, moving us to believe the movie business has become morally corrupt.

More and more parents are nixing movies in theatres for their children because violence and semi-porn have increased in the movie world, which is unfortunate movie makers accept this as normal in the film business today. To put us off more, ticket prices have zoomed to ridiculously inflated amounts and popcorn and drinks at the concession counter might cost as much as a steak dinner out! Seriously, this indicates a family of four might expect to spend upwards of a $100.00 for tickets and food for a movie out at the theatre.

What happened? Movie theatres were once a refuge, beloved, a happy, exciting place to go, fun entertainment we've loved since childhood. Our first Disney and cartoon movies with lovable creatures and characters gave us joy and lifelong memories. As teens we often indulged in a first stolen kiss, fell in love with glamorous and handsome movie stars, swooned over rock stars and knew the joy of our first fantasy crush. Screaming, laughing, and singing along took us to another world where we often wished or dreamed we could be them.

Going to a movie theatre to hang out with friends, escape from the blistering heat in cool air conditioning was a summer pastime, our flight into fantasy. Movies gave us leisurely activity, an opportunity to indulge into a world to dream, collect memories with friends, and be close to our idols.

Thank goodness for progress, we now have all sorts of options with satellite TV and viewing technology beaming across the heavens allowing us to watch somewhere near ten-thousand movies in our home. Any category ever dreamed up is ours to choose for a fraction of the cost of a movie ticket, enjoyed comfortably at home, or anywhere we choose. Another perk, we can adjust the volume.

Recently, I succumbed to my husband's plea to go out to a movie; it would be a date night, see a newly released movie with one of his idols he wanted desperately to see. That is where I made a disappointing choice, I agreed to his suggestion; go out to a movie theatre.

We arrived at the ticket office 30 minutes before scheduled previews began because he wanted to get a good seat. We were stunned, the line at the ticket booth was nearly a half block long; the line for popcorn and drinks longer. Unfortunately, we learned the sting of waiting could have been avoided if we had purchased tickets in advance online.

To sum up our date night; uncomfortable and disappointing. Multiply happenings that took place put us off taking in another movie anytime soon at a theatre. Not only did we not get a good seat, the theatre was packed shoulder to shoulder, the previews were shocking, distasteful, certainly not for tender young ears or eyes who would have been there. Sound effects for gunfire and explosions were so loud they could blast open a gold mine if used instead of dynamite; possibly contribute to hearing loss!

But the gunfire and blowing up any and everything, lots of blood, screaming, foul, cussing language, horribly loud music, along with mediocre acting sealed it for me.

The most intolerable and annoying put off was other movie goers continuously talking on their cell phones. This most likely means the possibility of my stepping inside a movie theatre ever again is slim to none. What a shame.

The moral of this story: Sometimes sentimental memories and movie idols, are best left in the past.

And the Winner Is?

Awards are given freely for nearly everything today, which can be both good and not so good. Rewarding someone for an accomplishment deserving recognition makes a statement worth commending. But, it appears we have gone beyond legitimate awards for a job well done, crossing the finish line first, achieving a goal or the near impossible should be acknowledged. But there are people receiving awards for doing nothing! I'm not kidding.

Winning is a moving experience, humbling to receive recognition for something well done, work one has completed successfully, or a skill achieved beyond expectations. But today, awards and accolades are being given for simply attempting to accomplish something. This has come about because the _Whiners League of Losers_ are demanding they receive an award for participating in a task, contest, or sport for simply taking part or showing up to watch. It's true!

Why and how is this happening? Well, those from the league named above feel every endeavor should be rewarded, be given immediate attention with a prize, a certificate of some type, a trophy for showing up. They are even demanding a prize be given for attempting to accomplish a task but didn't! This has tarnished winning, which just isn't right.

The practice has been taking place in our schools, communities both small and large, at sporting events, and in organizations for some time. Several damand-ee's have become obsessed, determined and anxious to reward anyone for minimal effort in anything! This attitude to diminish good should give us pause, alarmed for the fact little effort is needed for anyone to be awarded an immediate prize for doing little to nothing.

Somewhere along the way parents, teachers, and others, usually chronic complainers, have stated we can't hurt the feelings of those who participated by not giving them a prize. They are asking for a prize for appearing at a competition even when they put forth or exercised little to no effort in the event. That is ludicrous, the fact anyone has the right to an award or trophy for being in a place even if they didn't try to win, didn't finish an assignment, the race, or didn't accomplish a thing. What a crock because they expected, demanded, and apparently needed some type of honor or trophy to appease them for not winning. This is beyond insane.

Prizes or trophies are given to those who work to achieve, which should motivate, not appease for being around to watch or possibly think of competing at any level. Awards or trophies should be given to the best in competition, not to anyone who simply showed up and thought of competing. How difficult is this to figure out?

This should apply to the workplace as well; unfortunately, the film/movie/music industry has begun to give awards for daily participation no matter if anything was completed, much less accomplished or stood out on merit. Apparently, those who have become preoccupied with the idea of equality, feel everyone is entitled to the same award or prize, everyone is the same, identical. This outlook is unbelievable, way over the edge of reality.

It's good to receive praise, feel the long hours of practice, research, or hard work paid off. So, what are those equality sissy's telling us? Hard work and discipline is no longer important, everyone should be treated equally even if they didn't do equal work? Are they trying to convince us that self-esteem is more important than ethical hard work, practice, or reaching goals? What is it then we are being rewarded for?

Is it possible those who want to give prizes and awards to anyone who shows up are groping for a platform? Are they trying to hog the limelight, or reason that it's only fair that everyone does not have to do well to be recognized? This seems to state that critics want everyone to be as mediocre as they are.

Are these beliefs being put into place by losers, those who have little discipline, have never worked toward a goal, never put in the hours it took to become proficient at a sport or task? Each of us should challenge all age groups, all social levels, provide tools so everyone will be able to know what accomplishment is, what a setback is, or why we have criticism, what is fair and honorable. It's the challenges and accomplishments that will take us far in life

The idea everyone should be a winner, every participant in any quest should and needs to be rewarded for little constitutes one does not have to do well to get recognized. This type of attitude will most likely do more harm than good, those who have done little will have few quests to prove to themselves and others. Nor will they be moved to earn or accomplish much. Winning or losing has been part of man's quest since time began, it prepares us for the realities of life in everything we seek.

Forget About It

I've talked about this so many times it's troubling; worried over what the outcome of my forgetfulness might come to. This could lead to seeking help on how to help myself remember things, places, and people forgotten.

Here's the situation, it's never been a secret I've been forgetful on occasion for years, parenthood can sometimes have that effect on the sharpest of minds. Although, while there are things and people I wish I could retrieve the memory of, there are others I'm quite happy I've forgotten. I can recall a few important aspects of the past vaguely, but it doesn't bother me that I can't remember what impact they had on my life. Which could be a good thing they are gone from memory; I'm fine knowing that forgetting isn't all that bad.

Still, there have been times I've wished I could remember a few people, events, and happy times from the past but I'm doing good just to hold onto what is in the present. This is referred to as old age forgetfulness, which is something I hate admitting, yet its consoling that my friends are also complaining about absentmindedness.

Of course, there are those who possess a good memory, but the fact is as we age, step into the golden years, it's just another thing we learn to deal with. There are medications, herbs, vitamins, and such we can try in order to improve our memory. However, I'm not sure I should spend half my life savings on pricey self-improvement techniques, praying they will help.

But here's the thing, I don't know why we forget; but it seems a clinical therapist who treats people with personal issues such as phobia's, addictions, and more has said forgetting is natural and helpful. Most people feel it's good to forget, especially those who believe leaving past craziness, odd people, or embarrassing things behind.

Not remembering every detail of our life can be healing too, so quit worrying over what can't or doesn't need to be recalled factually. It could also be a method for saving money if one forgets a few relatives, anniversaries, birthdays, and such. And, consider this, most of us have something we simply don't feel is worth remembering.

Mistakes made, stocks, investments, or houses not bought at a good price then sold where a ton of money could have been made is worth forgetting. We should want to forget the grief children and annoying relatives caused, money spent foolishly, and some of the stupid looking clothes bought because they were a fad; all should be joyfully forgotten.

Just how important is remembering people we dated, party friends hung out with years ago, and a few choices we made in clothing? For me, I can't recall there is that much, worthy of reminiscing over, especially people that would most likely be embarrassing. How about those clunker or ugly cars bought, or some of the awful furniture we chose, and how our house or apartment was decorated is certainly worth forgetting, especially that orange shag carpeting.

Books read, movies watched, concerts, plays, have slipped away too. It's possible they were either terrible, not worth holding onto, or dull and boring. I've met a number of famous people and politicians, but for some reason I remember little to nothing about them or why I was even in the same room with them. The weirdest thing, I have no idea what we talked about. This holds true to an awful job, miserable bosses, and co-workers, all reasons to be thankful to forget the trials of the workplace.

This should make me feel reflective, or possibly sad, but seriously, what I really feel is older because forgetfulness is a symptom of old age. However, I do console myself at times by believing I've known so many people and done so much that my mind is full. Retrieving anything that far back would be too much effort.

I also believe it's possible not much attention was given to everyday happenings, certain people, especially those not liked, barely knew, or had absolutely nothing in common with. The fact things or people are long forgotten probably indicates it's completely irrelevant, not worth bothering with. My advice, move on, accept forgetting could be, or is good for us.

Besides, facts from long ago or even last month have been altered, confused with other times, shoved aside for more important things. On the other hand, do we really want to know every detail of what happened, and is it worth retrieving?

Instructions and Warnings

Nearly everything in our home will need fixing or replacing at some time; upkeep and updates are a must for homeowners. This means purchases will be made over time for a few items, especially appliances for they simply wear out, break, or become so outdated they no longer work right.

Buying something new for the home is a feel-good type of experience, but most of us are disgracefully lacking in knowledge when it comes to installing a new item, or doing repairs. But the biggest deterrent are the instructions and warnings, which come with everything from a toaster to a faucet. Directions and warnings that will intimidate the purchase-ee to the point it's frightening.

The task of fixing or installing something at our home does take some ability and a load of patience, unfortunately, making sense out of the instructions confuses us to the point we doubt our self. Within minutes it's obvious the directions for the newly purchased item have been written by engineers who communicate on entirely different levels than the average homeowner. It's also possible they were assisted by the sky is falling, defeatist engineers and scientists who enjoy confusing us.

But it's the mandatory, issued warnings with new items, ordered by state laws, that muddle the mind and scare the consumer half to death. Even a NASA space engineer would be intimidated by the first line in the instruction booklet: WARNING: Read all instructions before installing or operating. Who reads ten pages of how to put an item together or how to operate it, then read two pages of warnings and disclaimers that come printed in fourteen languages!

If an attempt is made to decipher the instructions or warnings, immediate confusion will consume you. If you don't read them, ignore them all together, it's possible the item will never be used or work correctly. However, it is crucial they be read, but this is just scary what has been printed.

1. Do not immerse appliance in water while plugged in. 2. When leaving the appliance, turn it off. 3. Unplug item before cleaning. 4. Keep power off if replacing new blade. 5. Do not operate this product near explosives. 6. Choking hazard: Immediately dispose of packing material to prevent small children and pets from digesting them.

Just as frightening, which concerns me but I have to ask. What level of IQ customer is purchasing products for the home that a manufacture must print these warnings and instructions? 1. Keep electric cord off heated surfaces or flame. 2. Turn power button off before installing. 3. Keep hands and utensils out of disposal when turned on. 4. Do not allow children to operate power tools. Oh, my stars.

Most of us use commonsense and some knowledge when it comes to replacing and mending things, but these peculiar warnings are troubling. One in particular is odd; it advises the consumer not to cut open a battery because it has a poison substance in it. Who would do that, and why? Can you imagine what happened when these warnings were ignored? 1. Do not put hands or feet under or into mower when engine is running. 2. Engines emit carbon monoxide, do not operate in an enclosed area. 3. Turn engine off when not in use. Who doesn't know this? Why not?

Instruction booklets advise us if service is needed, contact the nearest factory center. Oh, please, the closest factory is usually in China! This means we will pay a local service business to repair the item we have abused, broken, or left out in the rain, or we did not purchase an extended warranty.

Unless you are extremely talented, can easily put puzzles together, and read instructions well, consider hiring a fix-it-do-it-all business trained to install or repair everything from an electric can opener to a backhoe.

Still, the way I see it, a project in a home should not begin without a first aid kit on hand.

A Word About Worrying

Remember when there wasn't a care in the world? We were children, time moved on, worry and concern creeped into the world with the most ridiculous of things. Passing a driver's license test, graduation, finding a job, and getting married. Today, the world is full of unnerving worries, concerns, and annoying circumstances.

Leaving home, or going somewhere offers the unexpected, however, its worrisome if we don't know what will be taking place, what poses a threat, or what unusual calamity might happen. What if the car breaks down, what if someone runs a stop sign and causes a wreck. See what I mean.

Staying at home brings us comfort, a safe place; or is it? A recent survey found that 46% of accidents happen in the home! People fall off a stepstool while changing a light bulb and break an ankle; or they slip and fall in the shower and wind up with a nasty cut requiring stitches.

Never in our history of mankind have so many experienced such overwhelming anxieties, concerns, and nightmares. Threats to our safety are with us daily in every form, which causes us worry throughout the day. We ask what will be recalled next on the vehicle we drive and who is trying to hack into our bank account

Threats to our health are shouted out on television, in magazines, and on the internet to the point we don't know what or who to believe. Dangerous chemicals and pollutants lurk in our air, food, and water, and oddly enough, in our mattresses and clothing. The world offers no safe place anywhere anymore, so it seems; according to television ads.

We are warned our toothbrushes harbor germs that can make us sick and our food and medications are sealed in near impenetrable plastic material to protect us from who knows what. Just as frightening, shadowy, unseen criminals are stealing identities twenty-four hours a day. Hurricanes, tornados, earthquakes, and floods tear our world apart and we are warned Aliens from outer space may launch an attack! Good Heavens!

The once enjoyed cigarette, pipe, and chewing tobacco can be deadly, gives us numerous health issues and alienates our friends. Too much sun will harm us, but the right amount is good for us! Drinking too much alcohol and coffee could pose a danger to our health, but drinking the right amount is good for our heart.

If a trip to the ATM after dark is necessary there is concern for an encounter with a mugger, getting a flat tire, or running out of gas, especially if on a deserted street after dark; it gives us the shivers. All are legitimate worries but the odds for them happening is slim; still the horror stories we see on TV and printed in the newspaper scares us half to death.

But the blue-ribbon champion worries are those that come after becoming a parent. Parenting worries begin the day your child is born and continue daily until the child marries. Parenthood brings on a whole set of worries, new anxieties and doubt that disrupt sleep for years, pushing one over the edge into sleep-depravation.

Home ownership gives us hand twisting worries, migraine headaches, and thoughts of running away from that home! Everything in the house will at some time break down or wear out, plus your vehicles will drive you nuts with ongoing malfunctions; each can deplete a bank account to create all sorts of financial worries and woes.

Working at a job to create an income and enjoy life is an entirely new set of worries. Will the promotion promised happen, will the boss fire half the staff to save money, will the company go bankrupt? The bills won't be paid, I could wind up homeless, my spouse might divorce me, and more! Just as frightening, I'll never find another job.

Driving anywhere is also worrisome, so is taking a vacation, or flying any distance, especially if you leave the country. When returning through customs, based on the uncertainty of the attitude of customs agents, could cause you to miss a connecting flight. On the drive home anxiety over the possibility your home was robbed while away makes us a nervous wreck. But even worse, has the computer been hacked and the bank account emptied!

Finding a qualified hairdresser or barber to keep our hair looking good is a concern, so is finding a dry cleaner that won't ruin or lose our clothes. It's possible most of us will never get the jump on fashion, psychologists will never have all the answers, and we can do nothing about the bland taste of hot house tomatoes. Nor is it possible to know if there is there enough saved and invested to retire comfortably?

Face it, there is a lot going on in the world, corruption, the stock market crashing, the cost of college, divorce, remarriage, death. Oh my God, what cemetery to go to, and what will the children do with everything in the house?

What if a meteorite crashes into earth, what kind of damage would it do? If extra-terrestrials visit, how would we communicate? What if all the money spent on vitamins didn't help, or the exercise equipment purchased didn't do a thing to keep us in shape or extend our life!

It's a terrible thing to waste a mind wondering about tomorrow, next month, or year. Should I purchase a driverless vehicle, or wing it with the old style one? Will crime take over the neighborhood, keep us locked behind security systems, gates, fences, and doors with impassable locks the rest of our life? Should I move?

The golden years are a crock too! If this is in fact the truth, maybe we should move to an island. Islanders are a happy bunch, no one living in a tropical setting, near and by the sea, seems to worry about much, they just chill out, relax most of the time. Not a care in the world

I don't know said this, but it sure makes sense. "If you can't change it or fix it, don't worry about it".

Are You Sure That's Right?

Before technology took over our lives we enjoyed a rather calm existence. We lived in houses with no or one bathroom, had no or one telephone, and computers were a thing of the future, right up there with going to the moon. Shortages of water and air wasn't even a thought. My, my, how things have changed.

There is no such thing today as a winner, dumb people seem to be taking over and we have thousands of variations in light bulbs to light up our life. We can repair or replace our teeth, knees, hearts, and fix our failing and ailing bodies.

Going on vacation can be frustrating, even dangerous, but living at home or dodging driverless cars could, and has, killed us. The weather has become as odd as a neighbor with security cameras and keep out signs posted about the property. Sadly, we are so scared and suspicious of so much we lock ourselves behind gates, fences, and sleep with an armed security system and guns.

Alarmist chill our spine with warnings of threats our world might explode into zillions of bits and pieces and float off into the black holes of the universe. And their prediction, we as a people will become extinct is nonsense, along with the doom and gloom they assure hangs over us daily. Why naysayers live in such a state is beyond reasoning, even psychics wouldn't promise such bunk.

Getting anyone to repair anything in or around our home sends us into fits while driving a vehicle or boarding an airplane to go anywhere requires nerves of steel and the patience of a saint. Just as trying, shopping for any fixture or appliance for our home can short-circuit our brain to the point we ask, why me!

Manners and thank you notes are a thing of the past, plus no one knows how to write anymore; or read it seems. Progress has stretched our nerves to the limit instead of making things easier and opening a package or getting a lid off anything requires special tools, expelling a few cuss words, and super strength.

However, believing the human race will become a number on the endangered list is just poppycock. Although, robots will probably wind up building and driving our vehicles; which will more than likely make us safer because we wouldn't be dodging a bunch of crazed drivers who have no idea what a speedometer is, or what a red light and stop sign means. It's a fact that driving America's highways scare and challenge us daily, brings on unexplainable nervousness, cussing, and mumbling, especially at drivers who are eating a meal, applying makeup, or talking on the phone while behind the wheel.

Our weather has gone wild, vacations sometimes exasperate us, and challenges facing us with home repairs freak us out. Still we ask, what happened to the working handy man, or to showing up at a scheduled time, to thoughtfulness, and common curtesy? Did unconcerned dumb people decide it wasn't necessary or why bother? Is rudeness a new way for inconsiderate people to thumb their nose with a na-na-na-na-na attitude. And shouldn't each of us try finding happiness in our world as opposed to being grouchy most of the time?

But the big question: Why are so many people trying to convince up to quit wasting time? How do they know how much time is being wasted, and what if that is exactly what some of us want to be doing? Advice: Take time to chill, rest your mind, relax with a time out well spent doing nothing or exactly what you want to; even wasting a bit of so-called time.

Perhaps a few whining souls could take a lesson from birds. They sing constantly, flitter about engaging with other birds and overall don't have a care in the world. Maybe humans should try this more often no matter if you can sing or not. At least hum a few tunes; if you can't then spend some leisurely time listening to music, it just might make things feel right.

Elevators, the Up and Down of Trust

Elevators have never been a place I'm comfortable in, but then most of us have at one time hesitated to use one. I simply don't trust them, use one only if it's an absolute necessity. This sounds like a phobia, which is okay, because I'm not alone with this fear. Thing is, the fear of elevators has come true.

During my youthful working years my office was in a downtown high rise on the twenty-second floor. I rode reluctantly shoulder to shoulder with dozens of other workers inside a metal box taking us to offices day after day. If there were odd creaking, grinding noises, or the car too full, people complained, some choose to get off, take the stairs; see, I wasn't alone.

In that building, in the elevator, was where I experienced every nightmare imagined could happen, did. It was an incident giving me reason to change jobs. One early winter morning I planned to work half day because weather predictions were grim for after three o'clock that day. Arriving early hoping to get some work done, then leave before predicted stormy weather would make the drive home difficult.

93

I entered the elevator with two co-workers who had the same plan as I. Within minutes it happened, the elevator groaned, jerked to a stop, alarm sounds rang out, and sirens were heard in the distance. The three of us were stuck between the seventh and eighth floor inside an elevator, the smell of smoke made a frightening statement; the building was on fire.

Within minutes fireman were on the eighth floor above us talking through the door and via an elevator phone. It would take about twenty minutes to move the cables manually, move the elevator in position, then open the doors to retrieve us. They advised us to sit on the floor and relax until they could get us out. Relax!

Every fear and uncertainty that had lingered for years, the edginess I'd felt each time I rode an elevator raced through my mind, at that moment, the nightmare of millions was mine. Inside a metal, six-foot by six-foot box suspended seven stories above street level, held there by a few cables, unmoving, inside a burning building with no way out.

My male co-workers sat on the floor and casually talked work stuff. I sat on the floor, my head laying on my arms across my knees, left me one choice, pray while my nerves shivered and shook. Thirty minutes later the slow, groaning elevator moved down to the 7th floor, the doors manually opened, fireman's hands helped us step out, said we were in no danger, then guided us through the stairwell and outside. I sat down on a bench with a medical person who questioned me. The fire was quickly contained on an upper floor, but the building would be closed.

To no one's surprise I took another job, vowing to never work in a building more than four stories high, using elevators reluctantly for more years than I want to admit. At times I was chided for taking the stairs to reach a destination, but I shrugged it off, the plus of my choice, I was getting daily exercise by taking the stairs.

Over time I learned there was an entire group of elevator passengers with stories on encounters, concerns, and fellow rider's odd behavior; some so comical or frightening they were worth retelling. Those stories ranged from personal experiences, people arguing, insulting each other, lawyers yelling at clients, to mothers with ill-behaved children, even a few fist fights.

The funniest of happenings were tales of smells endured, everything from dirty diaper stink, unwashed bodies and lunch smells, along with over indulged after shave and perfumes. The most common and worse; someone would release a gassy smell to permeate the already stale air, secretly let go with a silent, take-your-breath-away ill wind discharge.

If we think about it, movie makers should be blamed for feeding our fears of riding on elevators. Scenes showing killing people with guns, knives, poison gas, beating passengers up, robbing them, men in black suits and sunglasses, escorting someone off the elevator, to kidnapping. Then scenes of sabotaging the elevator where it breaks loose and crashes in an explosion on the bottom floor are keep you awake nightmares. See what I mean.

However, a pet peeve I had traveling in Europe was the lack of elevators. Europe has at least thirty-million stairs to climb if you want to visit a historical site, museum or art gallery, you will climb them all. Twenty-million are uneven or broken medieval stone steps. This is possibly their way of encouraging exercise, climbing, falling, and stumbling across the continent.

In my youth, time was spent traveling Europe, two days of my travels were spent in the Louvre Museum because, one, it is the size of New Jersey and two, it had no elevator. This encouraged moving to other floors via 1,680 steps! Throughout Italy, France, and Greece I climbed at least 14,000 steps to see some of the most famous museums and sites in the world. I left Europe exhausted because not a single elevator had been installed anywhere I visited.

Except that one lone elevator in France, which was in the Eiffel Tower. There I discovered, while stuffed in a four-foot by four-foot box, arm deodorant isn't a commonly used product by tourist. Given a choice of an elevator or stairs to leave the tower, and the magnificent sights of Paris, I chose the stairs, all 1,665 of them.

Argue with me, say elevators are newer, safer, high tech, sleek, and glide along effortlessly, no need for concern. Well, sometimes new things are made to look better than they are. My prediction; everything new or old will at some point break, elevators will always be suspect, scare us on occasion, and forever urge me to take the stairs.

Is That Real?

Life's pleasure is at hand every day in a variety of areas, but it seems way too much is fake, things that don't adhere to our expectations. So, we ask; why are there so many phony thing's in our stores and on line today? It's frustrating, makes shopping difficult, and puts us in a grouchy mood.

Faux this or that is everywhere, fake labels, knock off purses, copies, even imitation flavors and scents. It isn't exactly deceitful to make and sell reproductions and copies but it sure is maddening wading through the phony stuff to find the genuine item.

With so many fake articles for purchase we take up an extensive search to find an authentic leather chair, not a fake vinyl, or a pair of genuine leather shoes. It's gotten to the point of near trickery in our quest for the authentic. Window blinds and floors come in faux wood, imitation bottles of perfume draw us in, and lab created diamonds are everywhere; items we must examine closely to document they are genuinely fake.

I personally have issues with someone selling knock off designer purses touted as the real thing. It's downright deceitful, cheating. But I'm fine with adding false eyelashes or fake hair extensions to our existing hair style, or wearing a wig or hairpiece to look good. And I'm good with adding fake fingernails, especially when it's tough to keep the real ones looking perfect.

Because a real diamond is quite pricy some consumers are okay with the lab made, which is good because there are those who can't afford the real thing. But it's not good when we set out to buy a beautiful, real ruby, a precious stone mined from the earth, then discover it's a lab created stone; we have been had, duped!

If a fashionable piece of clothing or coat is labeled faux fur, we may buy it for several reasons, usually because we like it and it's a fashion statement. I can also accept fake leather purses labeled vegan, which is good because that's a humane choice. Just don't try to convince me these items are real.

However, I'm not a fan of fake crab meat. True, it's cheaper than the real thing, and it is real fish, it's the fact a man-made flavoring has been added to real white fish to make it taste like crab meat. This makes me wonder how the flavoring is made? Just as important, is it made with some odd additive we shouldn't be eating?

We know there is fake news out there, but it becomes frightening when its learned journalist deliberately make news up to confuse and trick the general public. It's also quite alarming to know thieves are working round the clock to steal our identity and pretend they are us.

What about fake flowers? I'm sure they are wonderful for certain uses, but I personally don't want them at my funeral. Just as bad, forgers are out there every day using someone else's name to do all kinds of dastardly deeds. Worse; crooks are constantly finding new ways to make and print counterfeit money, fake ID's, credit cards, and documents of all types!

Unfortunately, there are con-artists, card sharks, and deceptive types using every imaginable shim-sham to deceive us. This is nothing new, crooks have been doing this for centuries. But this is just as scary; we're pushed beyond our wits end dealing with phony people pretending to be something or someone they aren't. Sadly, it's become a way of life for some, which is downright annoying!

This isn't new, but it's still maddening; even our coffee has been highjacked. A couple of coffee companies took it upon themselves, some years back, to give us coffee in an instant. Fake coffee in the form of a freeze-dried process that takes away the whole idea of enjoying rich, fresh brewed coffee to wake up our senses and body. What a crock, anti-pleasure, punishment, an assault on our taste buds and thinking process.

No one should be subjected to such a vile taste for its the worse, uncivilized measure to fooling the public. Especially when trying to wake up, stumbling to the kitchen half asleep, in need of a reviving cup of steaming coffee, not some fake granules colored brown with a chemical disguised as a coffee flavor.

There will always be fake stuff, phonies, con people, and imitations in all sorts of things, I can live with that. Just don't mess with my fresh brewed, steaming cup of real coffee.

The Truth About Spice the Dog

Spice is a dog, but believes wholeheartedly she is human, or at least the spirit of one. She isn't ordinary as far as dogs, or even humans go, rather like the Elizabeth Taylor of dogs, absolutely mesmerizing to gaze upon. Don't snicker, it's true; I, for a few moments, considered renaming her Elizabeth but as a very young puppy she was into everything, an adorable, very energetic, and spicy little girl.

Her coal black eyes could melt a glacier, her snow-white hair is beautiful and soft, and her nails perfectly clipped at the grooming spa where she has a standing appointment once a month. She is, to say the least, pampered like a princess and has such a sweet, happy personality she can only be described as eight pounds of charming, irresistible love.

Two of her best, rather famous traits; she is a champion kisser and licker with the energy of a three-year old toddler, believing everyone in her presence is her playmate and every place is her playground. She plays hard all morning then immediately lays down in her bed for a two-hour nap. She dreams like an angel because she is champion snoozer resting upon a memory foam mattress covered with a cashmere blanket and a downy-silk pillow. Only the best for little miss prissy princess.

She loves treats, begs constantly for them, gobbles up her gourmet prepared meals, drinks only filtered water, and loves her bacon flavored chew sticks. Unfortunately, Spice will never be a model of diplomacy when guests visit her home, she seldom takes no for an answer or follows commands of sit or no. Still, she is given attention befitting a rare Renoir painting or the accolades of a rock star.

Spice isn't interested in mastering any tricks, but she can sit, lie down, roll over, loves being scratched, is a champion tail wager, and an Olympic tug-of-war player. She loves her toys, takes them everywhere, outside, in the car, and to bed. Her specialties are amazing, definitely a top-notch attention getter, master snuggler and bed hog.

As watch dogs go, Spice is one of the world's most fierce barkers; barks at every foot stepping on her walkway, the mail delivery woman, and every FedX delivery truck that dares enter the street. She barks at every squirrel setting a paw on the deck and the neighborhood cat walking near the house, neither pay any attention at all, yet they scamper away after she yips and howls for five minutes. I'm sure they get tired of hearing her and just move on.

She loves to chew on shoes, purses, grocery bags, of course her toys, and is a major toilet paper shredder, it must be the lavender scent. She would win a prize as the best at chewing ball point pens, sunglasses, note pad, anything from nightstands, out of recycle bins or trash, from tables, and of course sticks from outside. I'm sure if she could laugh out loud, she would, filling every day with contagious laughter.

But as cute, intelligent, and loving as Spice is she intimidates her sister Sugar by taking over all the toys, eating Sugars food and stealing her treats. She hogs the sleeping space, jumps on Sugar when she is napping, pushes her aside so she can be the first to dash through the doggie-door to play outside, and overall annoys Sugar with an attitude of look at me first, I'm cuter. Still she has the personality you can't help but adore because she so loving, happy, cute, and energetic, similar to an actress seeking ongoing attention.

The magic of Spice, she is a loyal companion, listens intently at every word spoken by her humans. She never notices if her human unwittingly ignores her before a first cup of coffee or is poorly dressed. Nor does she mind if they are late to arrive home, late with her dinner, snore at night, or commit a faux pas. She loves her human companions unconditionally, and is the most affectionate, loyal friend, never stingy with her kisses, and always excited when they come home.

Parenthood is overrated, the accolades are long and ingenious, however, the pleasures of Spice the dog can never be summed up into words that would reveal the love within her, and the joy she brings to every day. She is truly priceless, regarded with the respect and love befitting the long reigning Queen Elizabeth of England.

Travel Tales from Americas Roadways

Americans love their cars, trucks, any form of motor transportation vehicles to the point they spend three times what their European cousins dole out on similar modes to get to and from. They idolize their cars, trucks, motorized bikes, and motor homes, race their cars, show their vehicles in a multitude of venues, and treat them as family members.

But it's the daily driving to work, vacations, transfers, and just getting things done while moving along roads and streets that will grind away at our mind. Why is that? Driving should be enjoyable, at least half the time, but we have drivers as varied as fish in the sea. Some on the road careening carelessly without a care in the world, lost, angry, stressed, scaring half the normal, careful drivers to death, erasing the pleasure we should have with driving.

Today, motorist taking to the roadways aren't paying attention to much or following the rules for sharing the roads. They are distracted, confused, or dead tired and sleep deprived. Just as scary, quite a few have never passed a driver's test, much less studied a driver's education manual, nor do they pay attention to rules, laws, and signage on the roads. Others are judgement-disadvantaged, some are frazzled mothers driving with small children.

I was once a stressed and frazzled, tired mother driving with small children and teens. Thankfully, I survived and give credit to my own parents who believed in the teaching of rules to live in society peacefully and productively. Just as important, they taught proper driving manners and lessons to navigate our roadways.

At the age of twelve I began driving, not on the roadways, that didn't come until I was fifteen so by the time I was sixteen I had fairly good skills. It was then I set out on as a proud graduate of driver's education classes and a state issued driver's license, confident with my new skills and authorization. By age eighteen I thought I knew everything, considered myself a good driver, however, navigating skills were challenging.

My driving and navigating skills were put to new challenge as the wife of a career Marine and new mom. I would take to Americas highways coast to coast and north and south for over twenty-five years. As a mother, I drove with children for long periods of time traveling long distances across several states. This presented an entirely new responsibility not easily explained to anyone who didn't travel much by automobile with small children, especially traveling hundreds of miles a day.

To my surprise, there was no manual for such a challenge, nothing regarding map reading, unmarked roads, farm roads, or rude drivers encountered in confusing city traffic. Nothing to warn of the dangers driving in fog, sleet, ice, or snow and often in torrential rainstorms when the children were either crying, fighting, or bouncing about the car. Nor was there one hint how to deal with pitfalls such as flat tires, dead batteries, small animals darting across the road, or children throwing up. These situations tried nerves to the breaking point.

The search for a self-help drivers manual to deal with the obstacles thrown at me went on for years as I traveled from state to state. However, the most stressful chore was to learn how to safely set out alone anywhere with children, which covered a time frame from birth to high school graduation.

Those youthful parenting years were lonesome times as I drove mile after mile, sometimes in blissful silence as the children slept. But it was the ongoing noise that eroded my nerves as years passed, time spent traveling with children, chauffeuring them to one function after another, lastly, teaching them to drive. This proved to be the biggest hurdle I'd ever experience, possibly the reason I'm now considered a nervous, but skilled, cautious driver.

During those years I experienced "Oh my God" flashing lights on the dash, broken away exhaust pipe dragging behind the car, dead batteries, steaming radiators, confusing road signs and highway numbering systems that changed in every state. Traveling across deserts and mountains had their own challenges and going through or around a city was grueling, the fastest way to erode every nerve in your body is to drive through any city at rush hour.

There were trying miscalculations that caused us to get lost in places few would want to be for any length of time. A horrific windstorm with blinding dust was the cause of a wrong turn into a part of town I swear had to be from a movie set straight out of the wild west. Tumble weeds were blowing about the street, several stuck against what appeared to be abandoned stores and buildings, giving the appearance of an old western town preparing for a gun-fighters shootout.

Without streetlights I couldn't tell where I was, too scared to stop so I just kept driving, eventually finding a street that led to a more populated part of town. The children asked questions why we were driving when we couldn't see out the windows, but the oddest of our travels and finding our way was a night spent in a roadside rest area.

After hours of driving without seeing a motel for nearly a hundred miles, a stop was made at a roadside rest area around midnight. Feeling very unsafe on a highway I didn't know where it would end I prepared the children to sleep in the car. The experience forever etched in my mind as something no mother should endure. How was I to know sleeping in a car with two young children, who acted as if they were hooked up to batteries, cannot be considered sleeping.

A decent night's sleep evaded me for it was more like nodding off every fifteen minutes before answering a serious of questions from the children. "Why do we have to sleep here? When can we leave? What is that noise? When can we eat? Can you turn the lights on, I'm scared? She's hogging the blanket. I have to go to the bathroom now!"

My experience traveling south of the Mason Dixon line was another unforgettable adventure. Of course, we were lost again because a number of roads in the south were not marked properly, stopping to ask directions from a local person was a must but nearly as confusing as being lost.

Listening to a man speak while chewing tobacco, giving directions how to find the interstate, was daunting to say the least. I felt as if I were teetering on the edge of a meltdown in south Mississippi, struggling to understand directions spoken in a slow dialect that confirmed our significant geographical and cultural difference.

Being lost in a city was worse. Had I have known I'd get lost to the point I'd find myself, with children in places we shouldn't have been, sometimes in abandoned warehouse districts, neighborhoods with stripped cars sitting like skeletons, or on dead end streets, and once in what was considered a red-light district. We also got scared half to death one pitch black night in an area with no street lights, cars and taxi's passing our vehicle as they careened about like drunks staggering, honking horns, apparently because we were going the speed limit, to slow for them.

No amount of training could have prepared me for what I would endure over the years, from the 1960's through the 1980's, traveling across America with children because of military transfers for my husband. The children ate and fought constantly, and they throw up for no reason at all, usually without warning, along straight highways and curving mountain roads alike. And they need to pee every 30 miles! They fussed and argued over toys, books, food, pillows, which usually had me shouting out threats, for some reason this didn't work because my children suffered hearing loss when they were in the car.

The constant nerve draining behavior of my normally well-behaved children was similar to an adult on speed! Plus, children never shut up, it was as if they ran on batteries with no off switch, even with threats, promises, and wait until your dad finds out. Nothing worked.

And for God's sake, and to keep yourself out of jail, never travel with children and pets in the same vehicle for more than three hours. We traveled with gerbils, dogs, fish, a lizard, and two parakeets in a cage. How my children came up with the idea that pets had to travel with us, plus like chocolate is beyond me. On at least two occasions one of the children fed the dog half a chocolate bar.

Dogs can't eat chocolate, they throw up in the car, on at least one child, then they get the worst case of diarrhea you or your vet hasn't even seen! You'll spend at least an hour at a gas station, with people staring at you, while you hose out the car's interior and scream at your children as you wash away the poop and vomit. From that day on, the car will always smell like pet throw up, which is similar to the faint scent of skunk; I'm not kidding.

It's exasperating washing that kind of mess and stink off a kid in a gas station sink or in a roadside park bathroom, an experience no mother should have to endure more than once; which I did. It was at this point in my life I must have become more religious for I found myself praying more, especially asking "Lord, please help me" or "Jesus, please don't let me kill one of them".

Because I had to travel often without my husband, I sometimes put the children in charge of getting us from point A to point B on the map. One child became the co-navigator, or as we named it, "riding shotgun", giving them a helpful job. On several occasions, the navigator got distracted, confused, or would fall asleep. They were pretty good for seven-year old's, which is when I began asking them to help, apparently map reading was tough, this made me ask why it couldn't be a required learning program in school.

They did get pretty good at reading road signs, when they paid attention, however, all of us needed more help with the road atlas, especially when we couldn't find the town we were supposed to be driving through! This did happen on several occasions; usually at night. Reading or making sense of road signs during the day was difficult enough but at night it was tricky, to say the least, especially when the children fell asleep.

To preserve my fragile sanity, I learned to never depend on the locals or a convenience store cashier to give directions or point out a location on a map. The locals think everyone is from the area, so they give directions such as: "Drive down here about two miles, as they point, turn east at the stop sign and go about a mile, turn north at the water tower, go past the old Mullen place, turn down that street and it will be right in front of you."

I finally had to accept my children suffered hearing loss in the short distance between the time the door closed to the house and my starting the engine for the car. They never heard me say, over and over, "No we can't stop again, we just stopped." Still they begged because an advertising billboard appeared every five miles for something they wanted to see or do. We did stop at several places that were not on the agenda because I couldn't stand the screaming and crying accusing me of ruining their vacation.

We can laugh now when reminiscing about long-ago car trips; stopping at nearly every historical marker in every state, remembering our regrettable encounter with a snake. And, of course the potty stops made every fifty miles or less. It was a given one of them was always "going to throw up right now", no wonder we got such poor gas mileage, for we seemed to stop and start a dozen times a day. I will confirm this applies to several states; the yellow-stained, dead grass along the highway wasn't from the drought, it's a result from the children's emergency potty stops because the constant shout out was, "I can't hold it any longer"!

Because of our near poverty level budget for long trips, I packed food and drinks to handle the fact that children eat constantly when traveling. It was sheer hell. One child wanted mayonnaise on their sandwich, the other mustard, one only drank chocolate milk, while the other threw up if she drank milk period. I packed fruit, crackers, cookies and chips, and made peanut butter and jelly, peanut butter with no jelly, and bologna with no lettuce sandwiches; still the arguments were on who was eating what, and who was "eating everything or not sharing".

By the end of each trip, there were unusual smells drifting from the car moving you to ask why me. Getting rid of apple cores, banana peels, mustard, jelly, and other unidentifiable stains smeared throughout the car took hours; after one trip I resorted to taking a garden hose to the interior after we reached our destination. My husband would shake his head in grief by the sticky feeling to every knob, window, and handle he touched; obviously I didn't get the jelly, ice cream, and other sticky substances off everything.

I'm sure wherever our old vehicles are today, each of them still has a few cracker and cookie crumbs crunched into the carpet, and the bubblegum is still ground into the seats and floor. It wouldn't surprise me if sticky peanut butter and jelly was still under the seats and pee stains were still visible on the carpet. Along with a faint, lingering smell similar to skunk was detected.

In between traveling America's highways with semi-yearly transfers, I could have qualified for a commercial chauffeur license. Daily trips to and from school functions, field trips, every sport event the school had for students, music lessons, band, cheerleading, scout events, and 4-H functions and meetings. They went back and forth to horseback riding lessons, horse shows and competitions, and more. I had so many experiences with driving children a week would be needed to record events and mishaps, as well as frightening and comical encounters.

The earth shifted; my children grew into teens, old enough to learn to drive, changing my life forever. The first thing they did was drive me crazier while learning to drive. As adults they got GPS devices! Hours of training in map reading and figuring out highway signs are loss to time, useless! They have flown the nest, still I find it difficult to get in the car for a trip to the supermarket, or anyplace more than five miles from the house without looking into the back seat to make sure seat belts are secured. Sometimes an odd feeling springs up, thinking I'll get half way to my destination and hear, "I can't hold it any longer."

NOTE: Carol and her daughters traveled Americas highways from 1960 through 1980, often without her Marine Corps husband, coast to coast, across the southern and northern roads and highways of the US, crossing the southwest desert and both Appalachian and Rocky Mountains more than once. She drove the coast of

California from San Diego to San Francisco for years; north into Idaho, Wyoming, Montana, on across the Midwest to Ohio, south through Kentucky, West Virginia, Virginia, and on to the southern states coast lines. In 1969 a transfer to England for a tour of duty had them driving England's roads and streets, in London and other cities, as well as into the most remote areas of England, Wales, and Scotland. Driving in such a historical and magical land as Great Britain left memories and adventurous experiences like none other; some on the varied roadways. Fog thick and scary, snow that wouldn't melt, and iced roads, streets and highways without ice melting products were as treacherous as driving into a river! But it was poor roadway lighting, or none, and the oddest of highway signage that could try the mind and stretch one's nerves to the point days were spent recovering from a road trip or an unusual encounter on Britain's roads.

Memories of Mother

This was written to preserve precious and funny memories of my mother's lacking driving skills. Her attempt at learning to drive, the years she took her children to and from, and her attitude toward getting from one place to another in a variety of vehicles from the late 1940's until 2000 is both a tribute to her efforts and her simply trudging on no matter the challenge. She experienced several mishaps across the years that resulted in nothing more than a few dents and scrapes, bruised ego, and comments of "oh well". She handled the events with such a charming manner and happy laugh, one had to commend her for what she genuinely strived to accomplish. This story has been printed in two other publications but because I dedicated this book to her it's here for another audience to enjoy.

The Imperfect Driver

My mother is a hero to me like none other, identical, yet different, to millions of mothers across the globe. Her love for her children, family values, how and when she grew up, gave her a respected standing with her family, the community, and her church.

She was born as the roaring twenties began, surviving the difficult depression years, blooming during the 1940's war years as she raised a family. She was a wisp of a young woman standing barely over five feet tall, yet had the strength, mentally and physical, of her brothers. She had beautiful, unforgettable blue-green eyes, dark chocolate brown hair and bore a striking resemblance to the famous 1940's movie star, Loretta Young.

Anything she put her mind to she did well, including plant and nurture a half acre garden year after year for as long as I remember, then she would can and put up what it produced. She could shoot a gun as well as any man; cook as if trained by the finest chef, and more resourceful than Martha Stewart ever thought of being. But, she was a dreadful driver.

She did the wash each Monday in an old wringer washer, scrubbing stains from clothes on a washboard, hanging it on clotheslines in both summer and winter. Tuesdays was set aside for ironing with the rest of the week cooking and cleaning our home from top to bottom. All summer she cared for and nurtured her children, setting then free to play after their chores were finished, pick berries, and roam the countryside, but they had to be home before dark.

Her community and family looked upon her as a good friend and a devoted wife and mother with a sense of humor and charm that endeared her to all. Beloved by her older brothers and sisters of whom she remained close until their deaths, her mother, a rather tenacious, colorful southern belle, was her best friend and ally who took on the discipline of we children for mother seldom spoke a cross word and if she did get pushed to the limit she made threats that somehow never came to be.

Unfortunately, the sheriff and his deputies were not mother's greatest fan's, they eventually stopped issuing tickets for her constant driving infractions. My dad simply made donations to the annual fund-raiser the Sheriff's office held each year.

Like so many young families my parents bought a house and acreage not long after World War II ended. Located ten miles outside of town meant a vehicle was a necessity, prompting my father to buy a used 1941 Chevrolet truck to get him to work and us into town.

With nothing but a two-lane highway and farms between us and the small town, mother had to learn to drive. Soon after moving to the country daddy began teaching her the basics so she could obtain a driver's license. She banged into the garage, hit out buildings, scared the animals, bent fences, and bumped into trees.

After weeks of lessons there was improvement in braking, shifting gears, and staying calm no matter the mishap or distraction. Daddy praised her, told her to do her best, I'm sure he prayed more after that.

Her driving didn't improve that much over the years, nor could Mother be described as a skilled driver but she persevered. During colder months or if it was raining, her children rode in the front with her, witness to her struggles with shifting gears, her feet barely reaching the gas and clutch pedals. In fair weather months we rode in the bed of the truck, but either place, we suffered bumps, scrapes, and scares. She often slammed on the brakes, swerved to avoid hitting small animals darting across the road, or bumped into something, yet maintaining control when the truck jerked and jumped when gears were shifted.

Thank goodness she successfully dodged roaming cows crossing the roadway and occasional deer darting in our path, which usually meant she swerved enough to run off the road. However, hundreds of unsuspecting raccoons, opossums, and squirrels, or occasional skunk were no match for her driving maneuvers.

Over the years, daddy bought newer and better vehicles, eventually purchasing the new automatic shift car as mother never quite mastered gear shifting at the same time using the clutch. Nor did she become proficient in the art of driving any vehicle without experiencing a mishap. None were serious, but they were constant, dents and scrapes here and there, running into ditches, or bumping another vehicle in a parking lot as she attempted backing out of spaces.

In 1954 daddy bought a '53 Chevrolet sedan with automatic shift for mother, it appeared as close to an armored tank as one could get. The doors closed with a decisive clunk, the engine thundered, and it usually bounced back with little damage each time she ran into something. Still, with mother at the wheel, it lasted but a few years for it seemed no vehicle was immune to her driving mishaps.

After I married and left home my sister's letters or phone conversations always included reference to mother, usually a story regarding mother's latest driving infractions. Any vehicle daddy purchased never lasted long for either the brakes wore out from overuse, or the cars was so banged up they looked as if they belonged in a junk yard.

Each election year until she was in her late seventies, mother drove to her volunteer job with the election commission, often returning home after dark, which was mother's weakest area for driving. Her odd maneuvers and tactics witnessed by neighbors, friends, and relatives, brought offers to drive next time, for she had either bumped into something, ran off the road, or hit small woods animals during the ten-mile trip home.

Mother's driving escapades became legendary in our county; friends or family offered rides to various outings in efforts to protect her, other drivers, and various targets that might be in her path. Still she drove until age eighty-two. I believe my sister and cousins secretly celebrated when she retired from driving. No longer strong enough to fight the ravages asthma had taken on her lungs, she died at age eighty-seven, mourned by family and the community she devoted her life to so faithfully.

Her life, grit, and escapades, along with her charming personality, could fill dozens of pages. She was religious enough to guarantee her place in heaven but tough enough at age seventy-eight to shoot a man in the leg with a forty-five while he was breaking into her home she had lived for over sixty years.

Memories of mother are blessings, joyful, interesting, unforgettable; her presence, her laugh, love, and advice are missed beyond what words can convey. Stories of her youth, her life as a young, devoted mother, her faith after losing her mother, husband, and siblings, seemed to give her strength and determination. But the tales and memories that bring belly laughs and tears are those remembered why she might be considered one of the worst drivers to ever take to the American roadways.

Carol Cook

Writing since her youth, Carol honed her skill in writer's workshops and night schools while raising children, at the same time staying gainfully employed. Years spent in school didn't yield a degree in anything, raising children gave her a nervous tic, and publishing seven books has helped her come closer to getting things right. Her essays of funny, touching, complaints on everyday life have appeared in dozens of newspapers and magazines, earning her a fan club. Relying on the odd, unaware, and interesting sorts who cross her path to deliver unending ideas, she writes with a tongue in cheek take on life's mysteries, illusions, the imperfect, and the annoying in our world. Each story gives us reason to laugh at life and our self. Born and raised in the farmlands of southern Ohio; moved to California and kept going. The wife of a Marine Corps Officer Carol moved twenty-two times in twenty-five years, living and traveling across thirty-nine states and seven countries. In the second act of her life she moved to Texas and married internationally accredited Architectural Illustrator and Watercolor Artist, Robert W. Cook.

website: https//carolcookwriter.com
carolbcook@metro411.net